THE AMAZING FELIX

EMILY ARNOLD MᶜCULLY

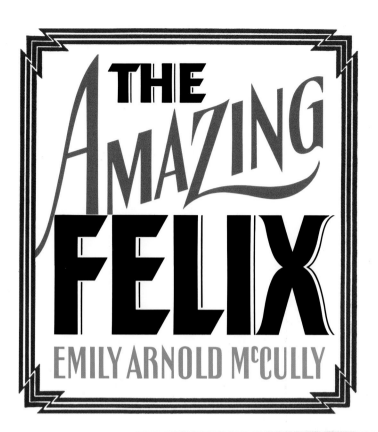

G.P. PUTNAM'S SONS · NEW YORK

Published simultaneously in Canada. Printed in Hong Kong by South China Printing Co (1988) Ltd. Book design by Nanette Stevenson and Colleen Flis. Lettering by David Gatti. The text is set in Bell. Library of Congress Cataloging-in-Publication Data McCully, Emily Arnold. The amazing Felix / by Emily Arnold McCully. p. cm. Summary: Felix has been practicing a magic trick instead of the piano and is worried about disappointing his musician father, but then he gets to be a hero in the castle where his father is performing. [1. Magic tricks–Fiction. 2. Musicians–Fiction. 3. Castles–Fiction.] I. Title. PZ7.M478415Mu 1993 92-10929 CIP AC [E]–dc20 ISBN 0-399-22428-9
1 3 5 7 9 10 8 6 4 2
First Impression

For Jake Dickerman

Even on the boat they had to practice. Felix could hear Fanny playing a Bach fugue over and over, no pedal.

Their papa, who was a great pianist, was about to finish a world tour. Felix and Fanny and their mother were to meet him in London for a holiday.

Months ago, as he was leaving, Papa had said, "Practice, practice, practice, children. When we are together again, I want *you* to make music for *me*. Fanny, no pedal on the Bach."

But no matter how hard Felix practiced, Fanny always practiced harder and played better. She would definitely make their papa happy. But would Felix? In only a week he would see Papa at last—and play for him. Felix felt a surge of joy—and a clap of dread!

When Fanny finally tired of practicing, Felix worked on his fingering. But what was the use? He was still stuck on the scales and exercises. They weren't music! It was too hard to sit still.

Felix roamed the boat looking for something—anything—to take his mind off the piano. But nothing he saw in the salons, the pool, the shuffleboard court or the skeet shoot seemed to help.

Then he came upon a little crowd.

A magician was performing a show, and it was astounding! Felix watched, not moving a muscle, but tingling all over with excitement.

After the last feat, he waited for the audience to leave.

"Señor Presto, that was fabulous! I want to be a magician too!"
he said.

"Call me Bert," the magician said. "I'll get you started with a trick.
Meet me on the bridge in half an hour."

Bert taught Felix to palm a coin. "Hold it there all day long, while you go about your business," Bert said. "It will become second nature. But you've got to practice, practice, practice!"

That was familiar. Felix did as he was told, palming the coin day and night. He even palmed it while he played his scales.

"Felix!" said Fanny. "That sounds dreadful. What on earth has come over you?"

She hadn't noticed that he was palming a coin! Encouraged, he practiced even more. Fanny practiced Bach's Prelude in C Major.

At dinner, the steward handed Mama a telegram. She read it aloud:
"'Darlings. Change of plan. Sir Basil Noble giving party in my honor
at his castle. Limousine to fetch you at dock. Can hardly wait. F&F:
Have you practiced? Love, Papa.' Well! What fun!"

"Oh, I shall adore to play for Papa at a castle!" Fanny said.

Felix imagined himself vanishing a coin for his father. When it fell out of his ear, Papa would be so amazed, he would forget to ask him to play the piano!

On the way to the castle, Fanny studied her scores. Felix palmed his coin, but he had a sinking feeling. Papa expected music, not magic....

When they arrived, Fanny shouted, "Papa, I practiced Bach with no pedal! Wait till you hear!"

"You're my angel," said Papa. "What about you, Felix?"

"I practiced too, Papa," said Felix. "Wait till you see! I have here an ordinary coin...."

"Maestro! We must go in." A man took Papa by the arm.

"I have to play for my supper," said Papa. "But then I will listen to you."

Inside, a party was going full swing.

"Don't just stand there," Fanny said. "Let's see what they have to eat."

"It looks disgusting," Felix said.

"This is caviar, you dope. Mama says it's a rare treat!"

"Well, I'm not hungry," said Felix.

"Now let's find some other children." Fanny sped away.

Before long, he heard her voice again.

"…my little brother." She spotted him. "Felix! This is Sedgie and Clarissa and Gorse. They are cousins of a duchess, and they know how to climb up into the tower! Come on!"

Well, it might be fun to see the tower of a castle, Felix thought. But he had to scramble to keep up. They flew from room to room.

When he saw his own face in a mirror, he stopped.

"I have here an ordinary coin…."

It was very reassuring to practice.

"Feeelix," came Fanny's faint, echoing call. He plunged ahead, hoping she wouldn't jump out from a corner and scare him, the way she did at home.

"Wowy zowy!" said Fanny, high above him.

Just as Felix reached the top step of an ancient stairway, a door shut in his face. There was a moment of silence. Then he heard thumps and muffled cries.

"Felix," wailed Fanny.

"Let me in," said Felix.

"We can't," Fanny said.

The door wouldn't budge. There seemed to be nothing he could do. It was eerie sitting alone on the cold, ancient steps.

Suddenly Fanny howled, "GET MAMA!"

"I don't know the way, Fanny," said Felix.

"GET MAMA AND PAPA QUICK!"

Felix peered down into the darkness.

"FELIX! I'M GOING TO THROW UP!"

"Oh dear," said Felix. He tried to remember all the twists and turns they had taken. Fanny groaned and pleaded, and now Sedgie and Clarissa and Gorse were also begging him to hurry.

He had to try!

"I have here an ordinary coin,"
he muttered.

MUSIC!

He could hear a piano!

It was Papa!

"Mama, Papa! Fanny is sick and locked in the tower. I was lost, but
I finally found you!"

"Naughty children," people said.

"Oh. I'm sorry to interrupt, Papa," Felix said.

"But you are a hero," said Papa. "How did you finally find us?"

"Magic," said Felix, "and then music."

"That's my boy," said Papa. He turned to the audience.

"I must rescue my daughter. But I will leave you in my son's hands. He practiced while I went around the world. Now he will perform for you."

Felix gulped. But he HAD practiced!

"Bravo!" cried people in the audience.
"Look at that!" said Papa. "Fantastic! I have always loved magic!"
"You have?"

"But Papa, you must practice, practice, practice!"

"Since I was a little boy like you and saw a magician perform, I have wanted to make a coin vanish!"

"I could teach you," said Felix. "With your fingers, it ought to be a cinch."

E

McCully, Emily Arnold

The amazing Felix